Book-e-Book Ltd
71-75 Shelton Street, Covent Garden, London, WC2H 9JQ
First Edition

Text Copyright ©Faye Carruthers 2023
Illustrations Copyright ©Hazel Mattheou 2023

A catalogue record for this book is available from the British Library.

ISBN 978-1-7395218-20

In the winter's chill, a red robin shone bright,

he spread his wings of warmth in the soft moonlight.

With a Santa's hat perched on his head,

he flapped his wings and here's what he said:

This book is dedicated to my family.
Thank you for standing by
me and believing in me.

I'm not Santa but I am here to spread cheer,

I'll help all from little mouse to big reindeer!

Anyone who needs help give me a shout,

I'll do what I can when I am about!"

He heard the whispers of those in need
and decided to perform a kindly deed.
With feathers so warm and a heart so kind,
he fluttered about - those in need to find.

Then little red robin heard a reindeer shout:

"I am lost, I can't find a way out!"

Poor reindeer had got confused by the Christmas sights,
and the big and bright car headlights!

"I've lost Santa and all the Christmas gifts,
but worse than that, I've lost the naughty and nice list!"

"Oh dear, oh dear" the robin sighed.

"Santa will be so angry!" the reindeer replied.

"Don't panic yet, we still have time,
we can always order another on Amazon Prime"

That list has been written from what we've seen and heard!"

"Right, let's get searching" the robin exclaimed.

"I last had it over there" the reindeer explained.

They searched in the dark, only the stars alight,

"THERE!!" Screamed Robin, giving Reindeer a fright.

Next to a road was the naughty and nice list,

not to mention a sack of Christmas gifts!

Breathing a huge sigh of relief they slumped to the floor,

before robin guided lost reindeer back to Santa's door.

"A merry Christmas to you" robin said with glee.

"And to you too" said reindeer happily.

Off Robin flew when he heard a mouse squeak.

"We are hungry, we feel so limp and weak."

Robin swooped in with a plan at the ready -

"I can help you mouse, just hold steady!"

Robin saw a warm and cosy house ahead -
he knew all the humans would be tucked up in bed.

With his little beak he nudged open the door,
and there lay cookies and mince pies on the floor.

"We can't eat those, they are for Santa!" the little mouse cried,

"I think we all know Santa has eaten enough!" Robin sighed -

"His belly is round and he has chins aplenty,

I can assure you his stomach is far from empty!"

And with that, little mouse and his little mouse babies nibbled and gnawed until they had full bellies.

A merry Christmas to you" Robin said with glee

"And to you too" said mouse gratefully.

Away little Robin flew with his heart content,

helping others is how Christmas should be spent.

In the silence of the night the snow began to fall,

as Robin puffed up his feathers he heard a loud call...

Ho! Ho! Ho! Jolly good you have that list, Reindeer!

We need to know who has been naughty or nice this year.

I'm looking forward to eating my tasty treats,

I haven't eaten all year, I could do with food to eat!"

Remember the robin, so tender and small,
who wishes a merry Christmas to one and all.

Here's wishing a happy Christmas to you,
and to all of your loved ones too.

BV - #0105 - 091123 - C34 - 297/210/3 - PB - 9602616000019 - Gloss Lamination